# RETURN OF THE JEDI

# EGMONT

*We bring stories to life*

This edition first published in Great Britain 2017
by Egmont UK Limited, The Yellow Building,
1 Nicholas Road, London W11 4AN.

© & TM 2017 Lucasfilm Ltd.

ISBN 978 0 6035 7420 7
68484/1
Printed in Estonia

To find more great *Star Wars* books, visit www.egmont.co.uk/starwars

Stay safe online. Any website addresses listed in this book are correct at the
time of going to print. However, Egmont is not responsible for content hosted by
third parties. Please be aware that online content can be subject to change and
websites can contain content that is unsuitable for children. We advise that all
children are supervised when using the internet.

# RETURN OF THE JEDI

Adapted by Geof Smith
Illustrated by Ron Cohee

# THIS BOOK BELONGS TO

------------------------------------

A great war rages between the evil Galactic Empire and the Rebel Alliance. The rebel hero Han Solo has been captured by the bounty hunter Boba Fett. Frozen in carbonite, Han is a trophy in the palace of the worm-like gangster Jabba the Hutt.

Luke Skywalker, the Jedi Knight, has a rescue plan. He sends R2-D2 and C-3PO to Jabba's lair on Tatooine as gifts.

A mysterious bounty hunter arrives to collect a reward for capturing Han's Wookiee co-pilot, Chewbacca.

The bounty hunter is really Princess Leia! Under cover of night, she frees Han from his icy prison. Unfortunately, Jabba's Gamorrean guards quickly capture them.

Soon after, Luke enters the palace and orders Jabba to release his
friends. A trapdoor springs open. Jabba shakes with laughter as Luke
falls into a dungeon! A mighty beast called a rancor attacks! Luke
crushes it with a giant gate.

To punish Luke and his friends, Jabba will feed them to the Sarlacc, a sand monster. It will digest them for a thousand years!

But just before Luke is about to be eaten . . .
he springs into action! R2-D2 tosses the Jedi his lightsaber. The heroes quickly defeat Jabba and his henchmen.

KA-BOOM!

Han knocks Boba Fett into the Sarlacc pit. BURP! Luke and his friends escape Jabba's barge as it explodes.

Across the galaxy, Luke's father, Darth Vader, is about to set an evil plot in motion. He is overseeing construction of a new Death Star – a battle station so powerful it will be able to destroy the rebels. A force shield generated on the nearby forest moon of Endor protects it. The Imperial Emperor tells Vader he wants Luke to join the Empire. "Together we can turn him to the dark side of the Force."

Luke flies his X-wing fighter to Dagobah to finish his Jedi training with Yoda. The wise old Jedi Master tells Luke he must confront Darth Vader. Just before Yoda fades away and becomes one with the Force, he whispers, "There is another Skywalker." Suddenly, the ghost of Obi-Wan Kenobi, Luke's first Jedi Master, appears. He reveals that Princess Leia is really Luke's sister!

Luke rejoins his friends on the rebel convoy in space.
The commander of the rebel fleet, Admiral Ackbar, has a plan to
destroy the new Death Star. Lando will lead the space attack in
the *Millennium Falcon*. Han, Luke and Leia will lead a strike
team to the moon of Endor to disable the force shield.

Soon Luke and his friends
land on Endor to complete their
mission. Scout troopers spot the
rebels and race away on speeder
bikes to warn the Empire.

Luke and Leia hop onto a speeder bike and chase the scout troopers. The rebels zip through the trees and quickly catch up.

Luke and Leia stop the Imperial scouts, but they become separated during the chase.

Lost, Leia meets a small, furry creature called an Ewok. His name is Wicket.

Luke rejoins Han and the rebel strike team. They are worried because Leia has not returned. But as the heroes set off to find the princess, they are trapped in a net! *Whoosh!* The rebels are captured by Ewoks!

Luke and Han are happy to find Leia safe and sound at the Ewoks' village. The creatures bow before C-3PO. They think he is a golden god! He tells the Ewoks stories of the Rebel Alliance's heroic struggles against the Empire. The Ewoks release Luke and his friends and agree to help fight the Imperial forces on their world.

At the controls of the *Millennium Falcon*, Lando and his co-pilot,
Nien Nunb, begin the rebel attack on the new Death Star. On Endor,
Han's team and the Ewoks prepare to destroy the shield generator.

The stormtroopers aren't prepared for enemies as small as the Ewoks. The Ewoks' simple traps made from logs and rocks overwhelm the Imperial walkers.

Han, Leia and Chewbacca storm the bunker and disable the shield! Lando can now destroy the Death Star.

Luke surrenders to Darth Vader. He thinks there is still good in his father. But Vader delivers Luke to the Emperor on the Death Star. The Emperor wants Luke to unleash his rage and join the dark side of the Force. He makes the young Jedi fight Darth Vader!

Vader and Luke duel.

Luke wins the battle but refuses to finish off his father. "If you will not be turned, you will be destroyed," the Emperor hisses. He shocks Luke with evil Force lightning from his fingers.

Darth Vader feels the good growing inside him. With the last of his strength, he rises up and heaves the Emperor into a deep reactor shaft!

The Death Star is about to be destroyed. Luke wants to save his father. "No," Vader whispers. "You already have."

Meanwhile, the battle rages in space. Evading lasers and zooming TIE fighters, Lando and Nien Nunb fly the *Millennium Falcon* deep into the Death Star.

BOOM!

They destroy the main reactor, and the giant station begins to collapse. The rebels speed away as the Death Star explodes!

The evil Empire is defeated! There is a celebration from Tatooine all the way to Endor.
The Ewoks sing and dance, and Chewbacca roars. R2-D2 beeps with joy.

Luke is happy the galaxy is safe – and the Force is at peace once again.

# THE END